Squid-napped!

READ ALL THE SHARK SCHOOL BOOKS!

#1: Deep-Sea Disaster

#2: Lights! Camera! Hammerhead!

COMING SOON

#4: The Boy Who Cried Shark

SHARK SCHOOL

Squid-napped!

#3

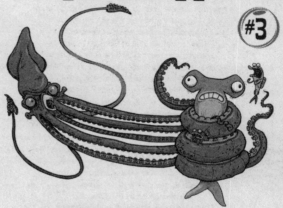

BY DAVY OCEAN
ILLUSTRATED BY AARON BLECHA

ALADDIN   New York   London   Toronto   Sydney   New Delhi

WITH THANKS TO PAUL EBBS

ALADDIN

An imprint of Simon & Schuster Children's Publishing Division
1230 Avenue of the Americas, New York, NY 10020
First Aladdin paperback edition September 2014
Text copyright © 2013 by Hothouse Fiction
Illustrations copyright © 2013 by Aaron Blecha
Originally published in 2013 in Great Britain as *Lone Shark* by Templar Publishing
Also available in an Aladdin hardcover edition.
All rights reserved, including the right of reproduction in whole or in part in any form.
ALADDIN is a trademark of Simon & Schuster, Inc., and related logo is a
registered trademark of Simon & Schuster, Inc.
For information about special discounts for bulk purchases, please contact
Simon & Schuster Special Sales at 1-866-506-1949 or business@simonandschuster.com.
The Simon & Schuster Speakers Bureau can bring authors to your live event. For more information or
to book an event contact the Simon & Schuster Speakers Bureau at 1-866-248-3049
or visit our website at www.simonspeakers.com.
Cover designed by Karin Paprocki
Interior designed by Mike Rosamilia
The text of this book was set in Write Demibd.
Manufactured in the United States of America 0814 OFF
2 4 6 8 10 9 7 5 3 1
Library of Congress Control Number 2014941350
ISBN 978-1-4814-0685-7 (hc)
ISBN 978-1-4814-0684-0 (pbk)
ISBN 978-1-4814-0686-4 (eBook)

CHAPTER 1

*Vrooooooooooooooooooooooooooooooo
ooooooooooooooom!*
*Vrooooooooooooooooooooooooooo
ooooooooooooooooooooooooooooooom!*
*Vrooooooooooooooooooooooooooo
oooooooooooooooooooooooooooooom!*
I'm floating at the side of Turbo Terry's

Turtle-kart Track as the turtle-karts whiz
past. It's making my hammerhead eyes
go double goggly.

"Don't look at me like that!' says Rick Reef, who is floating next to me. The pointy-faced reef shark (who is my number one enemy) waits until everyone is looking the other way,  then pings the side of my head with the edge of his fin.

"Hey-y-y-y-y-y! I can't help looking at you like that," I say, trying to stop my hammer from flubbering. "I have eyes on each side of my head! I look at everything—whether I want to or not. And in your case it's definitely *not*."

Rick pulls up the collar on his leather jacket. He always does this when he wants to look tough. "Yeah, but you don't have to be so starey about it."

"It's the turtle-karts. They're going so fast, they're making my eyes all weird."

Vroooooooooooooooooooooooooooooooooooooooooooooooooooooooooooooooom!

Vroooooooooooooooooooooooooooooooooooooooooooooooooooooooooooooom!

Vroooooooooooooooooooooooooooooooooooooooooooooooooooooooooooooom!

Three more turtle-karts zoom around the bend, their flippers whizzing like speedboat propellers and the electric eels underneath zapping up extra power for speed. Riders are hanging on to the turtle's backs with their fins or tentacles, all wearing brightly colored crash helmets with cool dragonfish or super squid cartoons on the side. I have to admit that this trip to Turbo Terry's Turtle-kart Track could have been really fantastic, if it hadn't been for five rotten things. . . .

1. It's my birthday. I hate my birthday. (No, really, I do. You'll see why later.)

2. Mom and Dad have taken us all to the turtle-kart track. (You think that's good? Think again, because . . .)

3. Mom and Dad are staying to watch! (How uncool is that? So uncool you can make hot sea-cucumber kebabs out of it.)

4. Everyone is noticing Dad because he's the mayor of Shark Point and he's telling everyone it's his number one son's birthday! (Daaaaaaaaaaaaaaad! Don't!)

5. And worst of all, Dad thought it was a good idea to invite my whole class—including Rick Reef (number one enemy) and Donny Dogfish (number one enemy's sidekick and general pain in the tail).

I did try to persuade Dad that Rick and Donny shouldn't come turtle-karting—in fact I've done nothing but try to persuade Dad ever since the invitations went out. Even this morning, when we were getting ready to leave, I tried again. But Dad was having none of it. "As mayor of Shark Point, I want everyone to get along," he said. "I know you and Rick don't see eye to eye, but maybe bringing him along today will be the start of a beautiful friendship."

Why do grown-ups say such weird things? There's nothing beautiful or friendly about someone who wants to flubber your head all the time.

FLUBBERRRRRRRR!!!!!!

See? He's done it again!

This time Rick pings my head so hard, my best friends Ralph and Joe have to grab hold of each side of the hammer to stop it from flubbering. Rick and Donny swim off toward the turtle-kart pits, snorting with laughter. It's nearly time for our session on the track to begin, but I'm really not in the mood now. I sigh loudly—so loud it makes a passing school of sardines dive for cover.

Why did I have to be born a hammer-head? Why couldn't I have been born a great white like my all-time hero Gregor the Gnasher? No one would make Gregor the Gnasher's head TWANG like a ruler on the side of a school desk—not without getting their bottom bitten off, anyway.

Gregor is the bravest, strongest shark who has ever lived. Not only is he

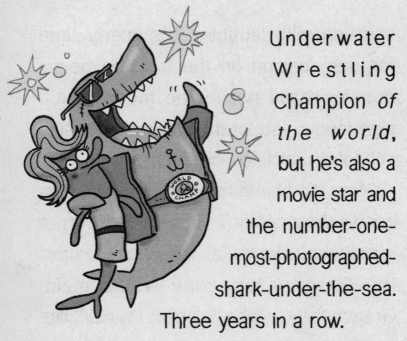

Underwater Wrestling Champion *of the world*, but he's also a movie star and the number-one-most-photographed-shark-under-the-sea. Three years in a row.

Ralph puts his fin on my shoulder. "Don't worry about it, Harry, just wait till we're in the karts. Rick'll be smiling on the other side of his face by the time we've beaten him on the track!"

I look at Ralph. Since he's only a pilot fish, it's hard to imagine him beating anyone on the track. He's too small to reach the controls, for a start, so we're going to have to share a kart.

I feel something quivering behind me and rotate my eyes to see my friend Joe. Joe is a jellyfish, and although he's not exactly a coward, he tries to avoid anything that might put him in danger. And since he's very good at finding out about stuff that might put him in danger, he ends up avoiding lots of things.

POP!

That's Joe thinking about karts. But

it's not his mouth that's popping, it's his backside. He does that when he's scared.

Ralph fins me in the ribs. "For Joe, karts equal farts."

Joe says, "You might laugh—"

(Which we do.)

"—but turtle-karting is the seventeenth most dangerous thing you can do on a Thursday."

"It's Saturday," Ralph points out.

"Whatever." Joe waves his tentacles around angrily, and turns a bit purple.

"Okay," I say. "Have we done the other sixteen more dangerous things today?"

Joe scratches his head with three of his thirty-six tentacles. "No."

"Then we'll be okay," I say.

"Come on, Harry!"

I turn and see Dad waving to me as he finishes signing autographs for a group of mirror carp.

"Time to get you on the track!"

I swim as slowly as I can toward the rickety old equipment shed next to the kart pits. I swim slowly because I know that soon everyone else will get really excited as they find the right racing jacket and fin gloves, but I'll just feel really embarrassed. The reason I'll

feel really embarrassed is because once everyone is in their gear, the pit chief, an old hermit crab called Nobbly, will start handing out the crash helmets.

I can feel my heart sinking like an anchor at the thought, and the water around my face warms up as my cheeks start to turn red.

Rick and Donny get cool helmets with dragonfish pictures. Ralph gets a supercool helmet with a pirate ship on either side and a skull and crossbones on the back. Even Joe's bottom stops tooting as Nobbly hands him a helmet shaped like a swordfish's head.

"Wow!" Joe says as his tentacles fight an imaginary duel with the swordfish. Then it's my turn.

"Oh," says Nobbly. "Hmmm. A hammerhead. . . ."

Nobbly starts searching the shelves for a helmet that will fit. I can hardly bear to look. I know exactly what's going to happen.

Rick and Donny are snickering in the corner—high-finning and using their fins to make hammer shapes on the sides of their helmets.

My cheeks are now so red you could use my face to warn ships about the rocks around Shark Point.

Nobbly looks at Mom and Dad. They just smile. Dad pats me on the head with a fatherly fin. "I'm sure they've got something in your size, son."

A few minutes later I'm not just embarrassed, I'm wishing the seabed would open up and swallow me whole.

"It's okay, I'll go with Joe—there'll be more room," says Ralph, trying really hard not to laugh. Behind me, I can hear Rick and Donny snickering again.

I watch as Ralph and Joe climb into their turtle-kart.

"It's not that bad, son." Dad says.

I just bite my lip and look straight ahead.

Nobbly couldn't find a single helmet to fit over my hammer head. So instead he found *two*! As I slide into the seat and Nobbly straps me in, I catch sight of myself reflected in the window of Turbo Terry's store.

I've got a helmet over *each end* of my hammer head. They're held in place by thick lengths of seaweed tape. But the seaweed tape doesn't cover the fact that both helmets are for babies and have pink cartoon starfish on them.

Bop-de-bop-de-bop-bop-bop! Shish! Shish! Shish!

That's Rick playing bongos on the two helmets while Donny dances around me, making cymbal noises out of the corner of his mouth.

"Enough of that, you two," says Nobbly, squeezing my fin protectively with his claw. Rick and Donny swim off to their turtle-karts. Trails of gigglebubbles stream from their mouths.

"Ready?" Nobbly asks, tickling the electric eel beneath my kart to get the turtle warmed up.

"Yes, I suppose so," I say through gritted teeth.

"Gentlefish!" shouts Nobbly. "*Start your engines!*"

And we're off!

Luckily, it isn't long before I forget about the double embarrassment of the double starfish helmets and actually start to enjoy myself.

The kart track is a figure eight with an over-under section in the middle. If I steer my turtle well, I can take it at full

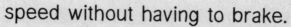

speed without having to brake.

Joe seems to be doing the best out of everyone. Because he has so many tentacles he can do about thirty-six things at once, so steering and braking at the same time is a breeze.

"Wheeeeeeeeeeeeeeeeeeeeeeeeee eeeeeeeeeeeeeeeee!" Joe yells with excitement as he races past the finish line, starting his second lap. Ralph is hanging on for dear life, but seems to be enjoying it too.

I overtake Donny easily and see Rick up ahead of me, just going around a bend. He's pushing the electric eel far too hard and the turtle-kart's gears are grinding in protest. The turtle itself is frowning up at Rick.

I tickle the eel in my kart and coax a little more speed out of the turtle. I'm starting to gain on Rick. I may be a hammerhead with two helmets and goggly eyes, but I'm not going to give up without a fight. I put my head down to reduce resistance against the water and flick my tail to give me a tiny bit of extra thrust. *You'd better watch out, Rick*, I say to myself. *You might be the fastest shark on the swimming team, but I'm going to prove I'm better than you at karting!*

Rick looks back over his shoulder and locks his eyes on me. I look straight back at him—as best as I can. Rick's face is all screwed up with determination, like there's no way he's going to let a hammerhead with two baby crash helmets strapped to his head get past. Yeah, well, having to wear two helmets is making me twice as determined to beat him.

I push on, continuing to catch up with Rick. When I'm almost on his tail, I see him look past me. I glance back and see that he's looking at Donny. Rick makes a signal to Donny with his tail. Donny suddenly turns his turtle and swerves around, going up the shoulder onto the upper section of the track—just as Joe and Ralph are coming past! Joe swerves and skids to a halt just before the crash barrier. Donny continues over the hump, across the other side, just as I round the corner about to overtake Rick.

Then I realize what is happening.
Donny's steered himself onto a collision
course with my turtle! There's nothing
I can do. Donny spears into the side of
me, sending me right off the track.

"You boys! Stop that at once!" Nobbly calls from the pits.

I turn the steering wheel with all my strength, but it's not enough. The turtle shell hits the crash barrier hard and we bounce back, straight into Donny. This pushes Donny into Rick and sends all three of us off the track.

KERRRRRRRRRRRR-ASH!!!!!!!!!!

The three turtle-karts spin to a halt and we lie there panting, trying to get our breath back, as Nobbly, Dad, and Mom dash over.

"Oh, my little starfish!" Mom wails.

"Are you okay, son?" Dad calls.

Nobbly tuts and mutters under his breath as he frees us from the turtle-karts, which immediately swim off in disgust. He chases after them to make sure they're okay.

"Have you hurt your hammer? Can

you swim in a straight line?" Mom cries.

"I'm fine, Mom! Don't have a sea cow." I wriggle as Mom hugs me and showers my two crash helmets with kisses.

"I think that's enough turtle-karting for today," says Dad, lifting me up off the seabed. "Time for your birthday party, I think."

I remove the helmets from each end of my hammer head and sigh. At least one thing's for sure—my party can't possibly go as badly as the turtle-karting. . . .

I have to sit at the head of the table in the restaurant. Dad is next to me, showing all his teeth in his best grin. This is because he's noticed the other diners nudging each other with their fins and whispering to each other that they're in the same restaurant as the mayor of Shark Point. Joe and Ralph are on my other side. Joe is gazing at the party food on the table in front of us. I know that the food is usually the best thing about a party, but not this party. In my head I start making a list of reasons why I don't want to eat it.

1. **Reef rolls**—there is NO way I'm eating anything that includes Rick's last name.

2. **Jelly-and-iceberg cream**—I'm not sure I can eat anything that reminds me of Joe, either.

3. **Rainbow-fish trifle**—the pink layer is exactly the same color as the awful baby helmets I had to wear.

4. **Sea-cow-cheese and sea-cucumber sandwiches**—cut by my mom into the shape of my hammer head. Great.

Ralph looks at my mouth. "Okay," he says. "Make sure you have some rolls, sandwiches, and trifle. I'm not excited about the jelly. It's really difficult for me to get it out from between your teeth, and even if I can get it out, it always dissolves before I can swallow it!" Ralph is a pilot fish, so he gets his food from the leftovers between my teeth.

Yes, it is as gross as it sounds.

"I thought it was *my* party food," I say to him out of the corner of my mouth.

"It might be your party food," Ralph hisses out of the corner of *his* mouth, "but it's *my* lunch."

I sigh and look down the table. Rick and Donny are at the other end. They're on their best behavior for once because of the scolding they got from Nobbly for causing the accident.

Mom is nowhere to be seen.

This makes my heart sink so low it feels like it's about to drop out of my tail. I know what's coming next and it's not going to be good.

I close my eyes and wish that I was a lone shark, like Gregor the Gnasher (when he's not busy being famous). If I was a lone shark, I wouldn't have to bother with birthday parties, because lone sharks never do anything in groups. And they definitely never have to invite their number one enemies to their birthday parties. *Maybe it won't be that bad this year*, I say to myself. But then . . .

1. The lights dim.
2. Music starts to play and the angelfish waiters form a choir around me and start singing "Happy Birthday" (except they sing "*Harry* Birthday"!).
3. Everyone in the restaurant stops eating and starts staring at me.
4. Mom appears, carrying an enormous birthday cake.

Mom. MOM! WHAT HAVE YOU DONE!?!?

Not only is the cake huge and fluffy and layered with sparkly rows of fish eggs, but Mom has also used the pinkest of pink-plankton icing to pipe two kissing sea horses on the top, and the whole thing is lit by a candlefish.

At the other end of the table, Rick and Donny start grinning so wide, a whale could swim down their throats.

Mom places the cake right in front of me. "There you are, gorgeous. Now blow your candlefish out and make a wish!"

With my cheeks glowing as pink as the cake, I lean forward to blow out the candlefish. The candlefish looks down at me and glares.

"You're a boy," he whispers.

I nod.

The candlefish shakes his head in disgust. "I've been stuck in all this horrible icing for a boy!"

I blow a stream of air bubbles into his face, but he stays upright.

"And why have you got two sea horses kissing on your cake?"

"I don't know," I hiss, blowing another stream of bubbles into his face.

But he keeps on complaining, standing upright in the icing. "You should've had two piranhas fighting."

"Be quiet!" I yell.

And then something truly terrible happens. I lean forward to push him over, but I lose my balance and topple forward, hammer head first, into the cake.

"Oh no!" Mom cries.

As I pull my head out of the cake, great clumps of plankton icing slide down my face.

"Harry's pink!" Rick yells.

"Like a girl," Donny says with a snicker.

"I'm out of here," the candlefish mutters as he swims for the door.

"Quick, make your wish," Mom says, dabbing at my head with a seaweed napkin.

I can't stand it anymore. This has been the worst birthday ever! Rick and Donny,

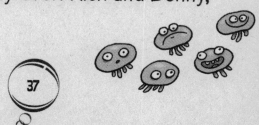

the dopey pink crash helmets, the dopey race, the dopey kart, and now the *dopey cake all over my face!*

"I wish"— I shout, getting up from the table—"I wish that it wasn't my birthday!"

Another piece of icing slides down my face and sticks to my top lip. Great. I'm wearing lipstick.

Rick and Donny can hardly float, they're laughing so hard.

There is a stunned silence. Then Mom begins to sniffle. "It took me ages to find pink plankton for the icing!" she wails.

Dad puts a fin around her.

I swim as fast as I can for the door. I just want to get away. Once I get outside the restaurant, I shake my head in the cooler water, trying to get rid of every last bit of icing. Ralph and Joe swim out behind me.

"Are you okay?" Ralph asks.

"No, I'm not okay!" I yell. "I've had

enough. Enough of Mom! Enough of Dad! Enough of Rick! Enough of Donny! And enough of my goofy head and everyone laughing at it!"

Joe pats me on the shoulder with about six of his tentacles. "Come on, Harry, it's not that bad. It's bad, yes, but not really, truly, awfully, terribly, humongously baddy-bad, like it is for me. I mean, you've only got three fins, a tail, and a hammer to find clothes for. Have you ever gone shopping with your mom and tried to find a hoodie with thirty-eight arms? No, you haven't. So things are much worse for me."

I shrug off Joe's tentacles. "But at least you only need one helmet. I've had enough! Lone sharks like Gregor the Gnasher have the right idea. They don't put up with moms and dads and double pink crash helmets and double-double pink cakes! No, they live in the open sea by themselves and do their own thing. No one bothers them, and they have a wonderful life!"

"But you're not a lone shark," says Ralph. "You're a hammerhead!"

That's when I have a brain wave. I look at him and start to smile, and my icing lipstick slides into my mouth. "Not for much longer. Starting tomorrow, I'm going to become a lone shark. I'm going to leave Shark Point for good and I'm going to go out into the ocean, and no one will ever be able to laugh at me again!"

CHAPTER 2

I'm swimming through the wide-open sea. I'm big, I'm brave, and I'm just like a great white. Not just any great white, though. I'm just like Gregor the Gnasher.

And just like Gregor, I'm leaving Shark Point behind, with cameras flashing and fish cheering my bravery.

"*Hurray! Hurray! Hurray!*" they shout as I swim and swim.

"*Hurray! Hum! Hurray! Hum! Hum! Hum!*"

I frown and stop swimming. Why are they saying "hum"? What's going on?

Oh.

I'm dreaming.

And the buzzing is Humphrey, my humming-fish alarm clock, trying to wake me.

I open one eye.

Humphrey pulls at my fin. "Come on, Harry, I've been humming for ages. If you didn't want to get up this early,

why did you tell me to wake you up now?"

I open my other eye but have to squint because Lenny, my lantern fish, is shining directly into it. "Come on, Harry!"

Lenny flashes on and off. "Time to rise and shine!"

I'm about to sigh when suddenly I remember.

Yes!

Today is the day I become a lone shark.

I launch myself out of bed and swim around the bedroom in my pajamas, looking in my drawers and under my bed for my cool Gregor the Gnasher T-shirt. When I've found it, I look at the list I made last night of things I need to take with me and start packing my back-pack. I can't wait!

LIST OF THINGS I NEED
TO BE A LONE SHARK

1. Gregor the Gnasher's autobiography. *Wrestling with Fame.*
2. Two packs of kelp krispies.
3. Uh ... ??? ???

"Harry! What are you doing?" Humphrey says, jumping out of my way as I swim around the room.

"I'm trying to pack," I say.

"But why are you trying to pack?" asks Lenny, with a concerned look on his face. "And why are you getting up before your mom and dad? You never get up before your mom and dad. Shall I go and—"

"No!" I zip to the door, slamming it shut and barring it with my fins. "No, I don't want you to wake them up, they'll only try to stop me."

Humphrey frowns at me. "Stop you from doing what?"

I put on my most serious face and say, "I'm leaving," as dramatically as I can.

Humphrey and Lenny both start to smile.

"Oh," says Lenny. "I thought it was something important. But you're just having one of your tantrums about being a hammerhead.

You'll be back by dinner. You always are."

"Not this time," I say. "This time, I'm going for good. You just watch."

Lenny and Humphrey laugh, and Humphrey winks at me. "Yeah, right. So, what time do you want us to wake you up tomorrow? You'll probably want a nice long sleep after all the huffing you're going to do today!"

Humphrey and Lenny chuckle and high-fin each other.

I glare at both of them and zip up my backpack. "You can *try* to wake me up anytime you like. Because I won't

be here!" I swim over to the window.

"See you later, then!" Humphrey calls as I swim away from the house. *I'll show them,* I think. *I can be a lone shark. No problem.*

The streetlights are still on, casting orange pools of light on the coral pavement. In the distance, I can hear the odd whale-truck rumbling through the morning water, and beyond that I catch the sound of the first turtle bus from Shark Point rolling out to Crabton.

Shark Point seems so calm and peaceful. So quiet and—

"Haaaaaaaaarrrrrrrryyyyyyyy!"

I leap up through the water in shock and turn to see Ralph and Joe speeding toward me. "Harry! Harry! Stop! Wait for us!" Ralph cries.

I shake my head and sigh. Honestly! How can you be a lone shark if no one will leave you alone?

"I was right, wasn't I?" Ralph says to Joe as they catch up with me. "I knew he'd get out early and try to give us the slip. Humphrey and Lenny were right—he *is* having a tantrum."

"*I am not having a tantrum!*" I shout.

Joe's bottom toots a couple of times

because he's a bit scared of shouting, and I hold up my fins.

"Look, I'm sorry. But I'm not having a tantrum this time, okay? I'm really doing this. I've packed, and I'm ready to head out into the open ocean to live the life of a lone shark."

"Show him the list," Ralph says, nudging Joe.

Joe nods and starts fiddling around with his tentacles. "I know it's here somewhere."

POP!

"Joe's been up all night, writing a list for you, haven't you, Joe?"

"Really?" I can't help being interested. I *love* lists.

Joe is still looking but manages a quick nod before turning a bit blue, then slightly purple, then completely green with embarrassment.

"This list," says Ralph, "shows you exactly why you shouldn't leave Shark Point. Right, Joe?"

Again, Joe turns, turns a little more green, and keeps looking. "Um . . . ," he says.

"This list has not two, not twenty,

not two hundred, but—count 'em—two hundred and forty-seven things on it that might go wrong for you out there!" Ralph announces. "Show him, Joe."

"Ummmmm."

Ralph frowns at him. "Come on, we're waiting."

"Ummmmm. . . ."

Ralph swims right up to Joe's ear and hisses, "Where's the list?"

"Ummmm." Bottom toot. Bottom toot. Bottom toot, toot, toot. "I think I've left it in my bedroom."

Ralph shakes his head. "Okay, Harry, wait there—we're going back to get the list."

I shake my head. "Look, I know you mean well, but I'm not interested in your list, not even if it has twenty-four thousand things on it. I'm going and that's it."

"You'll get lost! That's number forty-six, I think. . . ." says Joe desperately.

"I want to get lost!" I yell. "I want to get so lost I never come back!"

Joe turns white with fear. "But . . . y-you might get eaten!"

"Number eighty-seven," Ralph says.

I glare at them. "I'm a *shark.* I'm the one that does the eating. That's the way it works!"

Ralph holds up his fin. "But . . . but . . . where will I get my breakfast? I'm a pilot fish! You're leaving me to starve!"

I groan, undo my backpack and give Ralph one box of kelp krispies. "They should keep you going for a few days, until you find another shark to be friends with."

"But . . . !" Ralph and Joe shout.

"No! I'm going, and that's that. Don't follow me. You know I can outswim you both."

And with that, I tail-kick off down the street, stuffing fins into my eyes to rub, rub, and rub away the tears.

The town is fully awake now. Fish and turtles are coming out of their coral houses, on their way to work or school. I decide to keep to the back roads in case anyone else is out looking for me. I really hated saying good-bye to Ralph

and Joe, but it was for the best—I have to get away from Shark Point.

At the edge of town the buildings start to thin out, and my tummy flutters as I see the dark water of the open sea. I have to admit, I'm getting a bit nervous myself at the thought of striking out into the deep.

"Hey, Harry! What are you doing? Why aren't you on your way to school?"

I turn around. It's Cora and Pearl, the dolphin twins, and they're swimming toward me. They're holding their aqua-phones and typing away on them as they go, probably telling everyone on Plaice-book where I am.

"Look, I don't care what you say. I'm going! And you won't persuade me to stay!"

"What are you talking about?" asks Cora.

Oh.

"You haven't seen Ralph and Joe? You don't know that I'm leaving?"

They both look at their aqua-phones. "Nothing about it on Plaicebook," says Pearl.

"Oh. Well, I'm leaving Shark Point," I say. "I'm going out into the open ocean and I'm going to be a lone shark. I know you'll think it's a silly idea, but—"

"No, we don't," says Cora.

"It's an awesome idea," says Pearl. "You are sooooooo brave!"

Cora and Pearl hold up their aqua-phones and take pictures of me.

"Really?" I say. "I mean, yes, of course. It is a very brave thing to do, but hey, I am a very brave shark."

Cora nods.

I glance toward the dark ocean, and suddenly it doesn't feel quite so scary. I flex my dorsal muscles and wink at Cora and Pearl. "Wish me luck!"

As Cora and Pearl cheer me on and take more photos, I kick away from Shark Point and into the deep.

CHAPTER 3

It was all right being brave for Cora and Pearl, but pretty soon they're out of sight, and the view back to Shark Point is getting hazier. After a while, when I look back, all I can see is the same dark wall of water that I can see in front of me. And when I look down, it's even worse.

The sandy seabed I'm used to soon becomes huge boulders with deep, jagged cracks in them. Surrounding the boulders are tall forests of coral, their branches reaching spiky fingers high up into the inky blue water above.

"I'm not going back," I say out loud.

I say it out loud because the water here is so silent and it feels good to hear a voice—even if it is my own voice.

BOOM!!!

"What's that?" I yelp, spinning around. But it's too dark. I can't see anything.

BOOM!!! BOOOM!!!

BOOOOOOOOOOOOM!!!!!

I look down. Nothing. I look up. Still
nothing, just the weak light of the sun
 far above on
the surface of
the water.

"Hello?" I call
out again, my voice sounding all high-
pitched and girly. I'm not really expect-
ing a reply, I just want to use my mouth
to stop my teeth from chattering. So
when I do get a reply, I almost turn
inside out in fright.

"It's the whales breaching. Don't you
know nothin'?"

I can't see who's speaking. "W-w-whales?" I stutter, trying to make my voice less girly.

"Yeah," says the voice, right in my ear. *BOOOOOOOM!!!!* (That's the whales, apparently.)

TOOT! (That's my backside.)

The voice snickers.

"Humpback whales. Every time they jump out of the sea for some air, they crash back into the water and it makes that booming noise. You really don't know nothin' about nothin', do you?"

"Who are you?" I ask.

"Who I am doesn't matter."

I turn quickly and catch a flash of silver in my eye. I twist right; then, at the last second, left, into a perfect inside-outy. There, in front of me, is a minnow. Small and silver, with a rounded nose and a dark black line running down the middle of his body.

"Oooh, you're quick, Hammerface," says the minnow with a laugh. And with a *swish!* he's gone.

"Head!" I shout at the empty water. "It's Hammer*head!*" I pull a fast turn, and the minnow is in view. He sticks out his tongue and—*swish!*—he's gone again.

"If it's all the same," says the minnow in my ear, "I'll stay behind you. From the size of you, you're a kid—but you could still have me for breakfast!"

"I'd eat you even if it wasn't breakfast time!" I growl.

"Like to see you try."

"Would you?"

"Yeah."

"You asked for it!" I yell and throw myself into a triple dorsal spin.

GNASH!

My teeth chomp down on empty water and I hear the minnow snickering. I turn my head slightly so that I can swivel one eye back and catch sight of him. He's lounging on his side, covering a yawn with a feathery fin. "Too slow, chum."

SWISH! and the minnow is gone. *Again.*

I stop myself from charging at him without thinking. That won't work—this minnow is way too slick for that. And I'm a lone shark now. Lone sharks use cunning and guile when they hunt. Gregor the Gnasher wouldn't be chasing around after a minnow like this without a plan.

Trouble is, I don't have a plan. I decide to switch on my hammer-vision. Hammerheads have the best senses of any of the shark species because their heads are so big. It's like having a load of extra eyes that can see through stuff. But what's gonna help me now is the tiny vibrations I'll be able to sense as the minnow moves.

PING!

There he is! Using my fin-tips and tail, I quickly calculate the best route to take to head the minnow off.

My mouth waters and I can practically taste the fresh fish.

Mmmmmmm. Yum!

I wind up my tail, tense my muscles, and kick down.

I race through the water at top speed, my tail flapping furiously.

PING!

PING!

PING! . . .

. . . *GNASH!*

My teeth chomp onto empty, cold, unfishy water.

"You're so slow, I could tie your fins into bows without getting eaten," he calls out from behind me. "You must be one hungry shark if this is the way you hunt!"

Swish! In a flash he's in front of me, winking. "Is that your stomach I can hear rumbling?"

It's true, my stomach is rumbling, and I hadn't realized just how hungry I am. I think of the box of kelp krispies in my backpack. I'd much prefer a tasty minnow but there's no way I'm going to be able to catch this one. He's far too

tricky. And there's no point sticking around here to be laughed at. I could have stayed in Shark Point for that. I turn and begin to swim away.

"Aw, don't you want to play no more?"

I shake my head and keep swimming.

"I can teach you how to hunt if you like?"

The nerve! A tiny prey fish like a minnow telling me how to hunt! But I don't give him the satisfaction of seeing how annoyed I am.

I say nothing and swim on.

"Suit yourself!" says the minnow, "but don't say I didn't offer." And with another lightning *swish!* of his silvery tail, the minnow is gone.

I swim on alone, getting more and more down in the dumps.

This is hopeless. Maybe Humphrey and Lenny were right. Maybe I will be home for dinner this evening, with my tail between my fins and a whole world of embarrassment to face up to.

Maybe I'm not cut out to be a lone shark after all.

Then I see something move out of the corner of my eye. It's a big something. A really big something. I look down at the seabed. I can make out boulders and coral forests, sharp branches sticking up in the gloomy half-light. Then . . .

There it is again!

A shadow, huge and slow moving, rippling over the rocks.

Because of the lack of sunlight, I can only just make out a dim shape. Maybe it's one of the humpback whales I heard booming earlier.

Or maybe it's something else . . . something with sharper teeth.

Gulp.

But . . . what's that? Is it a dorsal fin? Is it the . . . nose . . . the pointy nose of a shark? *A great white shark?*

Suddenly I'm more excited than scared.

Of course! I'm out in the deep—this is prime hunting water for great whites. Maybe . . . maybe. . . .

No, it can't be. . . .

Can it?

Could it be Gregor the Gnasher?!

I pull down my T-shirt and smooth out the picture of Gregor. Oh man, if it is Gregor, I'll be able to get his autograph. Better than that, maybe Gregor could teach me how to hunt. And then I'll show that minnow who the best hunter in the sea is!

Kicking my tail, I swim down and down toward the shape, smiling the biggest smile I've smiled since before my disaster of a birthday.

Faster and faster and faster. . . .

"Gregor! Gregor! Hey! Wait! I'm your number one fan!"

And that's when I see that the shadow isn't Gregor the Gnasher at all, but I'm swimming too fast to stop.

And I *really* need to stop—more than anything in the whole world. Because I'm swimming straight toward the open tentacles and fearsome gaping mouth of a giant squid!

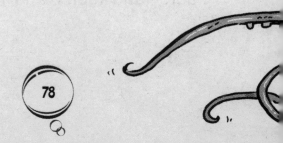

CHAPTER 4

I try everything I can to brake and change direction, but it's no good. I'm going way too fast.

And the giant squid really is *giant*!

It has about a million billion suckery arms, all twisting about in the water. Its

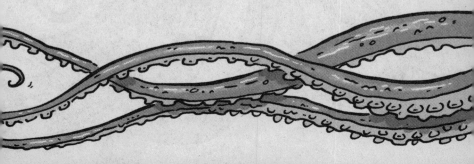

two big shiny black eyes, each as big as a turtle-kart, are staring right at me. And there, in the center of its huge, flat face, is the giant squid's mouth. It's deep, dark, and red, surrounded by a huge, razor-sharp beak!

How did I think this monster was Gregor the Gnasher?

The squid opens and shuts its beak really quickly, making a hissing sound like scissors cutting through sea- weed paper. He's showing me how deadly he is!

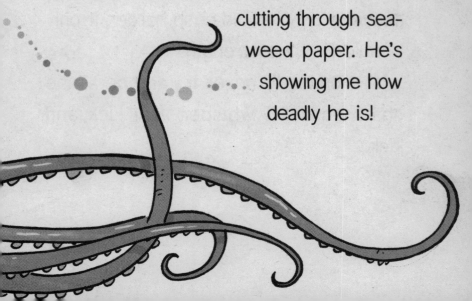

I push against the water hard with my fins. It takes all my strength to slow down even a little bit, and I could tail-flick myself for zooming down to the shadow without thinking of what could be lurking there. Oh, if only I'd listened to Joe and Ralph and stayed at home!

I push and push with my tail and feel myself start to slow. I look up to the dim surface of the ocean, many fathoms above. If only I could push harder, if only I could find the strength. . . .

"I promise I'll never try and be a lone shark again!" I whisper as I kick and kick.

It's working. I'm starting to slow down. I might just pull this off!

But that's when the giant squid shoots out his longest and suckeriest tentacle and grabs me right around the middle.

Puk!

Puk!

Puk!

That's the sound of the suckers attaching themselves to my skin.

I wriggle and twist, push and kick, snap and crunch my teeth, but I'm stuck fast.

"Let me go! Please! Let me go!"

The giant squid sucks the suckers

tighter and yanks me toward him, right up close to his hissing beak and huge, scary eyes.

"Let you go? Why would I let you go? I haven't had hammerhead in ages. Such a subtle flavor, the hammerhead. A reef shark or a great white can be tough and chewy, but a young hammerhead? Why, that's a taste to be savored, make no mistake!"

I gulp as the squid's mouth opens and closes and inside I see a thick purple tongue getting ready for some hammerheady flavors.

"I'm tough!" I yell, trying to break out

84

of the squid's grasp. "I'll stick in your throat. I'll give you indigestion! I'll make your breath smell!"

The squid hesitates for a moment. I think that maybe I've persuaded him not to eat me, but I'm wrong.

Another tentacle snaps out above my head, and I can see that it's holding a cookbook. Yet another tentacle starts to flip through the pages.

"Hmm, angelfish soufflé, crab cheesecake, grilled coral with a rack of sea squirt—that's a classic! Ah, here we are . . . hammerhead. Ooh, yes, that's just the ticket! Hammerhead Wellington with puffer fish pastry and a big splash of jellyfish gravy."

The squid sniffs up and down my body, making me shiver and shake, then licks his lips with his purple tongue. Ah, so fresh, so tasty, so alive . . . for now!"

I begin to struggle again, but all I'm doing is wearing myself out.

It's hopeless.

The squid gives a contented sigh as I go limp in his tentacles. "Ah, yes, so much better when lunch doesn't put up a fight."

Then he starts to swim down, carrying me like someone carrying their shopping home from the supermarket. I've never missed Shark Point so much in my life. I'm even missing Rick and Donny. What I wouldn't give right now to be wearing two pink crash helmets and to have Rick playing bongos on my hammer head. Anything would be better than this!

"Where are you taking me?"

"To my kitchen, of course," says the squid. "I need to cook you properly to make this meal the triumph I want it to be."

"Triumph? It's just lunch, isn't it?" I say sadly.

The squid stops dead in the water and looks at me. "Just lunch? Don't be silly, boy. Gordon Clamsey, Star Chef of the Seabed, doesn't do 'just lunch'! He creates menu masterpieces—he is an

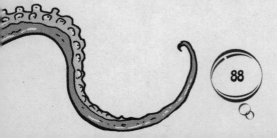

artist of the palate, a miracle worker of foodie wonder! You haven't been caught by just any old squid, you know."

I frown. "If you're a star chef, how come I've never heard of you?"

The squid shakes a few of his free tentacles in disgust. "It's not my fault those lame brains in Clam City aren't ready for a chef of my caliber in their hideous little restaurants. Thrown out just because I ate a few of the diners! I mean, what's a chef to do when he's a bit hungry and it's a slow day in the kitchen?"

"But a chef is supposed to feed the diners, not feed *on* them!"

"That's just what the restaurant owners said. Before I ate them."

My stomach flips over three times.

With a sniff and a ripple of his tentacles, Gordon Clamsey starts swimming down again. Soon the jagged boulder field that is the seafloor comes fully into view through the hazy blue water. Gordon pushes on toward a cave entrance. "Here we are, my boy!" he bellows. "Welcome to my kitchen, the place where the magic happens!"

As we squeeze through the narrow opening, he bangs my head against the roof. "*Ow!*" I yell.

"Just tenderizing the meat!" Gordon booms, with a hearty laugh that makes my eyes wobble.

Inside the cave it's almost completely dark. It's also dead cold, and I shiver. As my eyes adjust to the light, I wish that it was completely dark. The cave floor is covered in bones. Fish bones, crab shells, and the jawbones of sharks. I see one huge jaw with a rack of teeth that can only have come from a great white, a great white who must have been as big as Gregor. If a shark like that can't escape from Gordon Clamsey, what chance does a wimpy hammerhead like me have?

None. *Gulp!*

Gordon pushes me up against the wall and ties me to a rock with thick, sticky strands of seaweed.

Ugh! It's like being tied up with giant boogers!

Gordon swims back a little to admire his tentacle-work. He smiles and says, "Now, wait there. I'm off to get a few things to help you make my taste buds explode with delight. Stay fresh, now!" And with that Gordon leaves, and I'm all alone. Alone apart from the bones.

I jerk and strain in the cold, sticky grip of the seaweed but, like Gordon's suckered tentacles, it's far too strong for me to wiggle out of.

I think of how Rick and Donny would be killing themselves laughing if they knew how Harry the Lone Shark had found himself on Gordon Clamsey's menu as soon as he'd left town.

What about Joe and Ralph? How would they feel? They tried everything to make me stay and I didn't listen. They'll probably blame themselves. And Mom and Dad? Oh, man! Now I feel really bad. Especially when I think of how mean I was about my birthday cake. I feel so ashamed.

I have to get out of here.

I try shouting "Help!" a few times. But

the cave is probably too deep down. And if the locals know there is a huge killer squid chef living in a cave of bones, I hardly think any of them will try to rescue me.

I try to calm down a bit, but I can't get the thought of that huge, scissory, squiddy beak coming toward me out of my hammer head! I bite my lip. What should I do? What should I DO??????????

PING!

PING!

Huh? Why is my hammer-vision suddenly going off?

PING!

It's picking up movement outside the cave. Gordon must be coming back!

"Typical!" I groan. "Hammer-vision is supposed to show me the things *I* want to eat, not show me the things that are coming to eat me!"

I close my eyes as it gets even closer.

PING!

PING!!

PING!!!

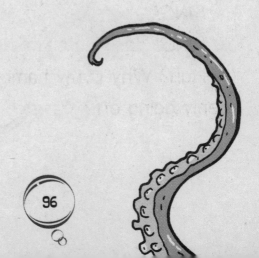

CHAPTER 5

"Yikes! You're in a pickle, aren'tcha?"

What?

I open one of my screwed-up eyes.

"What's up?" says the minnow. "You got time for a chat, or are you a bit tied up right now?" The minnow laughs his head off at his joke, even though

it's bad enough to be one of Dad's.

Then he comes up close to my face. "Thought it was you. I heard you yelling for help. You're not that brave for a lone shark, are you?"

I'm so pleased to see someone who isn't going to eat me that I don't care that the minnow's being mean.

"Get this stuff off me," I say.

The minnow looks at the sticky, boogerlike seaweed and makes a face. "You think I'm touching that? It looks like the squid sneezed on you."

"Please," I say, making my hammer-heady eyes as big and as appealing as I can. "You can nibble through it and I'll be free!"

The minnow shakes his head. "Listen, pal, there are two reasons I'm not going to get you out of that stuff. One, it looks like squid snot, and two, what's to stop you from eating me if I let you out, huh?"

"I promise I won't eat you."

"That's just what that fat great white, Gregor the Gnasher, said to my cousin Monty."

"Really?"

"Yep. Just before he ate him."

"Oh. Look, I don't know your name, and I'm sorry I tried to eat you before, but please help me. I promise I'm not like Gregor the Gnasher."

The minnow isn't listening. "See, if you don't wanna get caught by a giant squid, what you don't do is swim straight at one."

"I didn't know it was a giant squid!"

"Classic errors all the way, pal. Out in the open ocean? All alone? Error. Not really knowing what you're doing? Massive schoolshark error. Not even fast enough to overtake a minnow like me? Asking for major, error-y trouble, my friend. . . ."

"How does telling me that now help?"

The minnow nods his head. "Good point. Oh well, must be off. Places to be, sharks to annoy. . . ."

"Wait!"

"Why?" The minnow frowns at me. "We've pretty much covered everything. You're squid food and I'm off to have fun and *not* get eaten."

"Wait!" I plead. "If you won't get me out, please can you go to Shark Point and find my best friends Ralph and Joe? They'll come and rescue me!"

The minnow thinks for a moment. "And what's to stop this Ralph and Joe from eating me then, huh?"

"They're not sharks!" I say triumphantly, sure this will persuade the minnow.

"What are they, then?"

"Well, Ralph's a pilot fish and Joe's a jellyfish."

The minnow makes a disgusted face. "*Eeew!* Being a pilot fish has got to be

the worst job in the world. You wouldn't catch me eating stuff out of sharks' mouths!"

"Please! Will you go?"

But before the minnow has a chance to answer, we're startled by a suckery sound from outside the cave.

"It's hammerhead Wellington time!" calls Gordon's booming voice.

Swish!

The minnow vanishes.

Looks like I'm on my own.

Gordon enters the cave and grins. He waves a few tentacles around, bows as if he's in front of an audience, and holds up two shopping bags.

"You need three things to be a successful chef," says Gordon to the cave.

I look around to see if there are any

other squid who've come along to watch, but there aren't any. Perhaps Gordon just *thinks* he's talking to lots of other squid. I shiver some more. Being in the clutches of a killer chef is bad enough, but I'm in the clutches of a killer chef who's completely bonkers!

"First," continues Gordon, "you need the finest ingredients known to chef-kind!" Gordon empties the bags on the cave floor. I can see packets of dried jellyfish, bags of Piranha Puffs, and all kinds of weeds and spices. "Second, you need a kitchen worthy of your ingredients!" Gordon's tentacles shoot out in all

directions, and from the dark corners of the cave he drags a fancy captain's table (complete with red-checked tablecloth), a Coral and Limestone cooking stove connected to a sea gas canister, a huge number of shiny cooking utensils and, last, a clutch of sharp, evil knives.

I really don't like the way the blades glint in my ever-more-goggly eyes.

"And finally," bellows Gordon, throwing his tentacles wide, "the thing you need most of all is . . ."

I take a deep breath, terrified of what that last thing might be and how

it might be used to chop me into tiny pieces of shark sushi, or blend me into hammerhead-fin soup.

"The right hat!"

Huh?

Reaching up into the dark ceiling of the cave with two of his tentacles, Gordon brings down a huge white chef's hat. I look at it closely and see that it has been stitched together from several wrecked-ships' sails.

Gordon places the chef's hat on his head, like a mer-king putting on a crown. The puffy, mushroom-shaped top of the hat settles down and Gordon strikes a

pose, folding his tentacles one over the other over the other over the other over the other over the other over the other over the other over the other.

"And now," Gordon whispers, "we can begin!"

I try to push myself into the rock as Gordon picks up *one!, two!!, three!!!, four!!!!* of his sharpest knives and slowly makes his way toward me, licking at his razor-sharp beak with his leathery purple tongue.

CHAPTER 6

"*Wait!*" I scream as Gordon gets closer. "Wait! You've forgotten something really important!"

"No, I haven't," says Gordon, unconvinced. He looks around. "Ingredients. Check. Cooking stove. Check. Knives. Check, check, check, and check. Huge, floppy chef's hat. Check! Table. Check. Tablecloth. Checked. What else can I possibly need?"

Think of something! I say to myself. "You don't have . . ." *Come on!!! Come on!!!*

Then I have a brain wave. On all the cooking programs Mom watches, they're always going on about some- thing called seasoning.

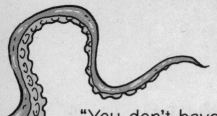

"You don't have the right seasoning!" I say with a gasp.

Gordon's chef's hat has fallen over the tops of his eyes. He pushes it back, scratches at his forehead with three spare tentacles, and peers at me. "I've got all the seasoning I need right here."

"No, you haven't!"

Gordon pushes his hat so far back that it falls off. He scrabbles around on the floor, picks it up, and puts it back on his head. "Look, you, zip it. Food should not answer back. Now, back to the matter at tentacle. . . ."

"Honestly, you don't have the right seasoning—for hammerheads you need . . ."

Think. Think. THINK! Yes!

". . . you need pink plankton. That's the best thing for hammerheads." I remember how it had taken Mom ages to find pink plankton for the icing on the top of my birthday cake. If I can convince Gordon to go looking for some, it might buy me some time. . . .

"Pink plankton?" Gordon eyes me suspiciously. "I've never heard anything about hammerheads and pink plankton before."

"It's true," I say. "I saw it on . . ."

THINK! What's that program Mom watches? ". . . Musselchef. Honestly, if you don't have pink plankton, I am going to taste really boring. And I wouldn't want to see a brilliant chef like you make such a huge mistake."

"Well. . . ."

Yes. Yes. Come on.

"All right."

SCORE!

Gordon sighs. "I'll go and find some, but when I come back, you're going in the pan and I am frying you up for lunch and then having leftover hammerhead sandwiches for later. Is that clear?"

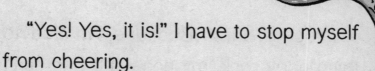

"Yes! Yes, it is!" I have to stop myself from cheering.

Still clutching the knives, Gordon turns around and swims out of the cave, grumbling to himself.

I know that this is my very last chance. If I don't get away now . . . I shiver at the horrible thought of being a giant squid's lunch (and dinner!).

The seaweed's too strong for me to get out of on my own, so if I'm going to get free, I'll have to find something that will help. *Okay. Concentrate. Find something. Anything* to get me out of this mess.

I look around. Because I'm tied to this dopey rock, my nose and fins can't reach any of the knives and utensils Gordon has left out on the table. I can't bend my neck to get my teeth working on the icky seaweed, either.

So what's left?

I look down and see that my tail is free. Great. That will be really helpful. Not.

But then . . .

I look beyond my tail to the floor of the cave. It's covered in bones and teeth and fish jaws. What if . . . ?

I *ping* on my hammer-vision and start scanning the cave floor. Look. Look. *Look!* Yes! There! Just in reach!

I start moving my tail. I swish it as hard and as fast as I can over the small patch of cave floor below me. Soon a huge cloud of sand and silt is rising into

the water. As I dangle, I'm uncovering more and more bones, and then, as the sand clears, I can see the edge of the cuttlefish bone I'd detected with my hammer-vision.

Cuttlefish bones are *razor*-sharp.

I push as hard against the seaweed as I can and wriggle my tail down a tiiiiiiiiiiiiiiiiiiny bit more. The tip of my tail just brushes the top of the exposed cuttlefish bone. That's a start!

I take a deep breath and squiggle down as hard and as far as I can. The bonds shift a little, and I can just . . .

YES!

My tail finally squirms under the cuttlefish bone and I flip it up.

The bone spins lazily into the water on a cloud of sand.

I reach out with my left fin.

Missed!

I lunge with my right fin.

Missed again!

The bone is still going up. I kick and kick, forcing myself against the snotty seaweed, and open my mouth to . . .

Chomp!

The cuttlefish bone is in my mouth. Luckily, not sharp-side up.

YES!

I tilt my head down to work on the seaweed.

The edge of the cuttlefish bone cuts through the sticky seaweed like a swordfish through sea-cow butter.

With a shake of my shoulders and a half-piked tail flip, I'm free of the snotty weed!

I shake the last pieces of seaweed

from my fins and kick away toward the entrance of the cave, and out into the dark water.

I've made it! I'm free!

Ping!

NO!

Ping!

NO!!

PING!!!

NO!!!!

My hammer-vision picks up a huge shape swimming toward me. A huge giant squid shape. Gordon Clamsey is back!

I thrust myself forward into

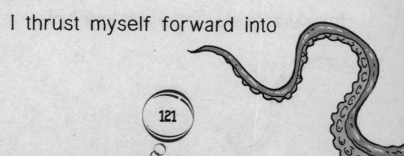

the water, back toward Shark Point, but I can feel from the currents in the water that he's getting closer.

"You tricked me!" Gordon shouts. 'You don't season hammerheads with pink plankton!"

"You don't?" I call back, swimming as fast as I can.

"No, and you know very well that you don't. I went to the library and got a kid-squid to look it up for me on the Interwet. And now," booms Gordon, "it's definitely *time for lunch!*"

"No. It's. Not!" I yell, swimming sharply from side to side to try and trick him.

"Oh. Yes. It. Is!"

Puk! One of Gordon's tentacles attaches itself to my back.

He starts to roll me toward his mouth.

"And I don't think I'll bother with the cooking," he says. "Sometimes food tastes best when it's RAW!"

I'm completely out of ideas. I'd set out to be a lone shark and ended up becoming a lunch shark. I close my eyes and hope it's over quickly.

"And what do you think you're doing with my little starfish?"

Mom?

I open my eyes. Gordon jumps in shock and lets me drop. I can't believe what I'm seeing either. There in front of us are Mom, Dad, Ralph, Joe, and a team of police sharks. A group of lantern fish are swimming in front of them, lighting the way. And in front of everyone is the minnow. He'd gone to get them after all!

"Mom! Dad! Ralph, Joe, and . . . umm . . . what *is* your name?"

The minnow looks sheep-ish. "It's not important, okay?"

Mom is advancing on Gordon. "I asked you

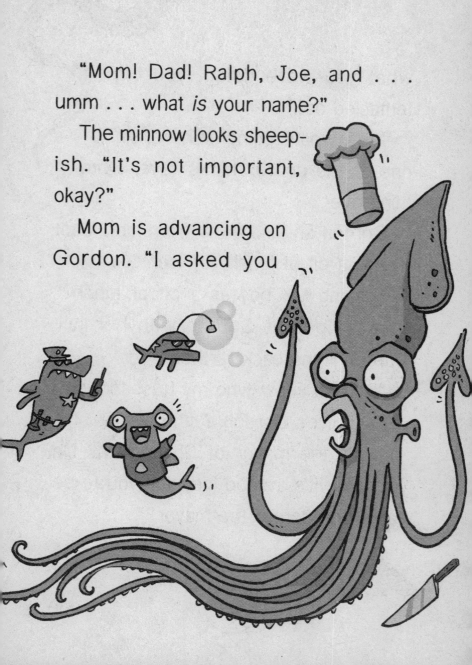

what you were doing, you big tentacled oaf!"

"Yes, what's going on here, sir?" one of the police sharks says, swimming over.

Gordon shrinks away from him. "Just having a bit of lunch, Officer. . . ."

"Having MY boy as a bit of lunch?" Mom swipes at Gordon with her tail. Gordon leans back farther.

"Do you know who my husband is?"

Dad gives Gordon a little wave.

"He's the mayor of Shark Point. Do you think it's a good idea for you to be eating the son of the mayor?"

Gordon shakes his head.

"It really isn't a good idea, sir," the police shark says. He clinks his pair of giant-size tentacle cuffs threateningly.

"We've heard all about you from this brave little minnow," Mom says. "The police know all about your job in Clam City, and we know why you were thrown out of that restau- rant. So I sug- gest you take my son off the menu or you'll have me, Mayor Hugo, and

every shark in Shark Point coming to turn you into *calamari*! Do I make myself clear?"

I can't believe what I'm seeing. Mom is scarier than Gregor the Gnasher!

Gordon nods and tries to hide his chef's hat behind his back. His tentacles start putting the knives inside his chef's jacket all on their own.

"Come on, Harry," says Mom. "It's time to go back home!"

I really don't mind being cuddled by Mom and Dad on the way back to Shark Point, even if it is in front of Ralph and Joe and my newest friend, the minnow. Mom insisted he come back to Shark Point for refreshments so she could say thank you.

As we approach the shallows around Shark Point, I turn to the minnow. "Listen, now that we're friends, you have to tell me your name. I can't keep calling you 'the minnow,' can I? It's silly."

"Not as silly as my name," the minnow says sadly. "You'll laugh at me."

"No, I won't," I promise. "How can I laugh at someone who's as fast and as clever and as brave as you? You're really cool."

"Not with a name like Marmaduke."

"Marmaduke?"

Marmaduke the Minnow nods.

I try not to laugh, but the bubbles from my nose show I'm swallowing a giggle.

Marmaduke frowns. "See, I told you you'd laugh! Well, I may have a silly name, but at least I don't have a head shaped like a novelty can opener."

I start to laugh out loud. Then Marmaduke does too. Then everyone laughs, except for Joe, who is being very, very quiet.

"What's up?" I ask him.

"My list of reasons not to leave Shark Point. It was garbage."

"Your list wasn't garbage," I say to him. "No way. It had two hundred and forty-seven things on it!"

"Yes, but none of those things was 'You'll get kidnapped by a crazy giant-squid chef'. That should have been in the top ten at least," Joe moans.

I laugh and pat Joe's jelly shoulder.

"Don't be sad. I'm just happy I've got such a brilliant friend who'd make a list that long to try to get me to stay. Shows me how lucky I *really* am!"

Joe smiles.

"So, do you still want to be a lone shark, Harry?" Dad asks as we swim into Shark Point.

I shake my head. "No way! The open ocean is way too dangerous for a hammerhead to be on his own. Especially one who tastes as nice as me!"

THE END

HARRY

Species:

hammerhead shark

You'll spot him . . .

using his special

hammer-vision

Favorite thing:

his Gregor the Gnasher

poster

Most likely to say:

"I wish I was a great white."

Most embarrassing moment: when Mom called him

her "little starfish" in front of all his friends

RALPH

Species:

pilot fish

You'll spot him . . .

eating the food

from between

Harry's teeth!

Favorite thing: shrimp Pop-Tarts

Most likely to say: "So, Harry, what's for

breakfast today?"

Most embarrassing moment: eating too much cake

on Joe's birthday. His face was COVERED in pink

plankton icing.

JOE

Species: jellyfish

You'll spot him . . . hiding behind Ralph and Harry, or behind his own tentacles

Favorite thing: his cave, since it's nice and safe

Most likely to say: "If we do this, we're going to end up as fish food. . . ."

Most embarrassing moment: whenever his rear goes *toot*, which is when he's scared. Which is all the time.

RICK

Species: blacktip reef
shark

You'll spot him . . .
bullying smaller fish
or showing off

Favorite thing: his
black leather jacket

Most likely to say: "Last one there's a sea snail!"

Most embarrassing moment:

none. Rick's far too cool to get embarrassed.

SHARK BITES

The dorsal fin is the main fin that is located on the back of a fish or marine (relating to the sea) animal.

Plankton can be plants or animals, but since they can't swim, they have to rely on the tides and currents of the ocean in order to move.

Sea cows are also known as manatees. They never leave the water, but since they are mammals, sea cows must come to the surface to breathe air.

Minnows can live in both salt water and fresh water.

Sharks have been swimming in the world's oceans for over 400 million years.

There are more than four hundred different species of sharks, from the giant hammerhead to the goblin shark.

Sharks do not have bones. They are cartilaginous fish, which means their skeletons are made of cartilage, not bone. Cartilage is a type of connective tissue that is softer than bone. Humans have cartilage in their ears and nose.

The shortfin mako is the fastest shark in the ocean. It can swim in bursts as fast as forty-six miles per hour.

The whale shark is the largest shark in the sea. It can grow to be as long as sixty feet.

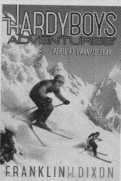

Join Zeus and his friends as they set off on the adventure of a lifetime.